SLEEP, SHEEP!

For my mom, Lynda Olsen, for always believing this was possible — K.L.S.

For Sassy, the dog who slept while I worked — G.P.

Kids Can Press gratefully acknowledges the financial support of the Government
of Ontario, through the Ontario Media Development Corporation; the Ontario
Arts Council; the Canada Council for the Arts; and the Government of Canada,
through the CBF, for our publishing activity.

Published in Canada and the U.S. by Kids Can Press Ltd.
25 Dockside Drive, Toronto, ON M5A 0B5

Kids Can Press is a Corus Entertainment Inc. company

www.kidscanpress.com

The artwork in this book was rendered in pencil crayon and colored in Photoshop.
The text is set in Catalina Clemente.

Edited by Yasemin Uçar
Designed by Guillaume Perreault and Michael Reis

Printed and bound in Shenzhen, China, in 3/2018 by C & C Offset

CM 18 0 9 8 7 6 5 4 3 2 1

Library and Archives Canada Cataloguing in Publication

Sparrow, Kerry Lyn, author
Sleep, sheep! / written by Kerry Lyn Sparrow ; illustrated by
Guillaume Perreault.

ISBN 978-1-77138-796-5 (hardcover)

I. Perreault, Guillaume, 1985–, illustrator II. Title.

PS8637.P374S64 2018   jC813'.6   C2017-907409-1

SLEEP, SHEEP!

Kerry Lyn Sparrow   Guillaume Perreault

Kids Can Press

Duncan liked bedtime snacks and bedtime stories.
He liked putting on his favorite pajamas. If there
was bubblegum-flavored toothpaste, Duncan even
liked brushing his teeth.

The only thing Duncan did not like about bedtime was going to sleep — and he would do anything he could to avoid it.

Duncan was pretty sure he knew enough tricks
to avoid going to sleep for the foreseeable future.

What he didn't know was that his mom
had a few tricks up her sleeve, too.

After his favorite bedtime story, Duncan's mom gave him a hug and a kiss and said, "Sweet dreams, Duncan."

"But I need —"

But Duncan couldn't think of anything, because everything he could possibly need was right there in his room.

"But I'm not sleepy!"
Duncan wailed.
"Try counting sheep,"
his mom suggested and
closed the door.

Duncan took a deep breath and
tried to think sheepy thoughts.
"One ..." he whispered.

To his surprise, a handsome sheep with a green
number one on his side jumped right over his bed!
Duncan rubbed his eyes.

"Two ..."

Another sheep, this one wearing a purple number
two with a matching scarf jumped over his bed.

Duncan looked around his room and saw that one side was crowded with sheep. They all wore numbers, like race cars.

Counting sheep was going to be more interesting than Duncan had thought! He fluffed up his pillow, pulled up his blanket and continued.

It was all going very well, and Duncan
was even starting to feel a bit sleepy
when he got to sixty-eight.

"Sixty-eight," said Duncan.
Sheep #68 stepped into position,
and then hesitated. Duncan paused his
counting and waited.
He waited and waited and waited.

Finally, he asked, "Is there a problem, number sixty-eight?"

Sheep #68 cleared his throat. "It's just ... well ... do you think I could have a drink of water before I jump?"

Duncan reached for the glass of
water that his mom had left and passed
it over to him.

When sheep #68 had emptied
the glass, Duncan said, "Ready?"

Sheep #68 nodded.
"Sixty-eight," Duncan said, and then waited.
He waited and waited and waited.
But sheep #68 didn't jump.

"Is there something else you need?" Duncan asked.
"It's just ... well, after all that water I really have to, you know ..."
Duncan sighed. "The bathroom is down the hall."

When sheep #68 returned, Duncan fixed him with a determined stare and said, "Sixty-eight ..."

Again, nothing happened.

"What now?" Duncan asked, exasperated.

"Well ... I'm just not sure I'm quite ready to jump yet. Maybe you could have a few of the other sheep jump first. Maybe I could jump after sheep number seventy-two?"

Duncan stared at him. "You want me to count 67, 69, 70, 71, 72, 68?"

Sheep #68 looked sheepish.

"I can't count like that," Duncan said. "It's your turn to jump now."

Sheep #68 thought he would like a bit of a run at the bed, so the other sheep cleared a path for him. But he put on the brakes at the last second.

Maybe he could use a step stool instead? No, he didn't feel comfortable about that. Maybe he should stretch first.

Or perhaps borrow sheep #23's running shoes? What if he took his socks off? No. What if he put his socks back on?

It went on and on like this, and still sheep #68 would not jump.

After drinking his third glass of water, sheep #68's eyes started to droop.

"Look," said Duncan. "You're tired." He pointed to the other side of his bed. "See how relaxed and comfortable those sixty-seven sheep are? Why don't you just join them?"

Sheep #68 yawned, heaved a big sigh and FINALLY made his way over to the other side of the bed.

Sheep #69, in his sleekest racing suit and extra-
springy sneakers, looked expectantly at Duncan ...
But Duncan was fast asleep.

Who knew that bedtime could be so exhausting?